THE SIDEMAN

THE SIDEMAN

Caro Ramsay

This first world edition published 2018
in Great Britain and the USA by
SEVERN HOUSE PUBLISHERS LTD of
Eardley House, 4 Uxbridge Street, London W8 7SY
Trade paperback edition first published
in Great Britain and the USA 2018 by
SEVERN HOUSE PUBLISHERS LTD

British Library Cataloguing in Publication Data
A CIP catalogue record for this title is available from the British Library.

ISBN-13: 978-0-7278-8808-2 (cased)
ISBN-13: 978-1-84751-935-1 (trade paper)
ISBN-13: 978-1-78010-990-9 (e-book)

All Severn House titles are printed on acid-free paper.

Severn House Publishers support the Forest Stewardship Council™ [FSC™],
the leading international forest certification organisation.
All our titles that are printed on FSC certified paper carry the FSC logo.

Typeset by Palimpsest Book Production Ltd.,
Falkirk, Stirlingshire, Scotland.
Printed and bound in Great Britain by
TJ International, Padstow, Cornwall.

PROLOGUE

Wednesday, 8th of November

Costello pulled her car up outside the big house. It looked cold and dead in the bright winter sunshine, rays glinted off the ivy-covered slates giving a sparkle to the bricks of the red chimneys. She looked at the stained-glass window, the multi-coloured mosaic of Botticelli's *Primavera* was just visible through the reaching branches of the monkey puzzle tree. Behind the tall wrought-iron gates the grass was verdant, the pebbles still raked into the neat furrows that had impressed Archie Walker. On that day.

That dreadful day.

The trees were tall and mature, even devoid of leaves they cast long spindly shadows over the wide road, old-fashioned, gently cambered. The kind of surface that leant itself to roller-skating, so Costello's granny had once told her.

She turned the Fiat's engine off, slipping down in the seat, thinking about the night she saw Malcolm try to climb out the window above the porch, attempting to get away from his father. And Costello was convinced that *was* exactly what the boy was doing. The message Malcolm had left on her phone? A twelve-year-old wanting help to escape from a monster.

She'd got the voicemail the following morning. When it was too late.

Six hours later Malcolm's body had been found in this house, curled up on the beige carpet at the foot of his parent's bed, his mother's arms still wrapped round him, holding him close, giving her only son some solace as his short life slipped away. No doubt her own last breath had swiftly followed.

That image was seared into Costello's memory, the bodies and the speckles and spatters of crimson blood on the mirrored wardrobe doors. She could recall the events up to that, walking into the house, opening the unlocked back door; the first warning sign. Then the music floating from above; 'The Clapping Song'. The element of theatre. Then upstairs past the little teardrop of blood on the magnolia wallpaper, the stain he thought he'd cleaned away. Then into Malcolm's bedroom, too quiet. The Star Wars posters on the walls, the smooth R2D2 duvet cover decorated with a Celtic top, a pair of black leggings, two woollen socks, the trainers. They were arranged as if the child had been lying there, dressed and then spirited away, shedding his clothes and leaving them behind.

In the car, Costello wiped an angry tear from her eye, remembering how she had paused on the top landing, alert to the smell of blood. She had hesitated, not wanting to go any further but the door of the master bedroom was open, intriguing and beguiling. And all the time that song was playing.

Clap clap.

Standing in the doorway she had seen the blood on the doors, the walls, the ceiling. She had to force herself to carry on; she gripped the steering wheel. It was hard to think past the iron-rich stench of the blood, the sweeter mulch of faecal matter. Her last memory was of Abigail lying curled, her arm up and over the smaller figure of her son; his hands wrapped round her elbow, his fingers still gripping the lilac silk of her blouse.

She had presumed she would have tomorrow to sort it out.

She had been wrong.

What would happen if she didn't act now? What if they ran out of time?

She looked back at the gates, closed now to keep the media away from the 'Monkey House Of Horror'. What secrets had those gates kept?

Costello had only to wait twenty minutes before she saw some movement through the bare branches of the beech hedge. She had been following George Haggerty for a couple of weeks; she knew his routine. He would be going north to see his father in Port MacDuff now. She slid down further in her seat as the garage door opened, the gates swinging wide, the white Volvo rolling out majestically to park on the street. The driver's door opened and Haggerty, casually dressed for him in jeans and anorak, got out and walked back up the driveway, his shoes making no noise or indent on the gravel. True to his routine, he re-emerged a couple of minutes later, locked the gates closed behind him and walked briskly back to the car where he stopped and turned. He looked straight at Costello and smiled, clapped his hands together slowly twice, and climbed into the car.

Clap clap.

He drove away, without looking back.

George Haggerty was getting away with murder.

And Costello was going to stop him, even if it killed her.

Or him.

ONE

The house on the terrace was quiet on a Saturday afternoon, all week it had been like Glasgow Central on Fair Friday, but everybody was out today. Colin Anderson had the whole house to himself. He was lying on the sofa, nursing a large Merlot and two sore feet after helping Brenda make an early start on the Christmas shopping. He was musing at the wine, as it swirled round the contours of the glass, admiring the patterns it left in the light of the wood-burning stove. His grandchild, Baby Moses, was asleep in his basket at Anderson's feet. Nesbit, the fat Staffie, was curled up on the sofa, ears tucked in so he didn't hear the rain battering against the windows. *American Beauty* played on the DVD, with the volume too low to hear.

It was almost perfect yet Anderson was not at peace. He was still digesting the news that his partner for twenty years had resigned. Costello was gone. No notice. No chat. No goodbyes. She had walked into ACC Mitchum's office unannounced, uninvited and slapped her letter of resignation on the desk right in front of him.

Just like that.

Twenty years they had worked together, fought, made up and fallen out again, shared laughs, heartache and a few broken bones. She had always had his back. He had always had hers. At times, their thinking was polar, opposite points of the compass, balancing each other into a relationship that while turbulent, was effective. Their track record proved that. Now she was gone. Brenda, his wife, had explained it simply. The events of the last few months had been too intense. Costello had found Archie Walker. Anderson had found Baby Moses.

Both of them had moved on and maybe George Haggerty had been the catalyst that finally separated them.

But then Brenda would say that. She had never really liked Costello.

He checked his phone. He was meeting the guys tomorrow for fish and chips, a long-standing arrangement. Costello had been invited. She had declined.

Anderson could accept that she had resigned in a fit of pique, saying she could do more about Haggerty without the restriction of the badge. She thought 'killing the bastard' would do her more good than any counselling.

And she had been furious when her request to form a task force to investigate the murders of Abigail and Malcolm Haggerty had been refused. The case had been transferred to Complaints and Internal Investigations, purely for clarity and transparency, but to him, and Costello, it felt they themselves were being scrutinized and judged. The first two people on the murder scene were members of the law enforcement community, and not just any members; a DI and Chief Procurator Fiscal. And as the fiscal's goddaughter was the victim's sister, the press were having a field day.

Haggerty was now talking to the media, playing on the 'Monkey House of Horror' crap. The case had rarely been out the papers for the last six weeks. Every day there was another tasty morsel revealed by the press. One thing they were all agreed on: the police weren't coming out of it well. George Haggerty was the obvious suspect and he was the one man who couldn't have done it. Even ACC Mitchum let slip that he too, had taken a very close look at that alibi. He had personally interviewed the two police officers who had caught Haggerty speeding in his white Volvo on the A9. One obvious suspect. Police Scotland were his alibi.

Yet, Costello had persisted that George Haggerty had killed his family.

He looked down at the bundle of pink skin in the Moses basket. His grandson, his link with Haggerty, the one reason they kept in touch. Anderson didn't like Haggerty, not the way his daughter Claire did. God, she had even drawn him a portrait of Baby Moses in pastel and had left it for him, signed and wrapped. Anderson wished she hadn't bothered. There was nothing he could define, nothing he could specify, just a very intense feeling of dislike. If he himself had one tiny piece of physical evidence against Haggerty, Anderson would have brought him in and every bone in his body would have told him that he had the right bloke. Every time, he was in Haggerty's company, Anderson could sense smirking guilt.

Anderson watched the Merlot, tipping it to the left and right. 'He has a watertight alibi,' he said out loud, 'and no motive at all.' He looked at his grandson, blowing bubbles in his basket. 'Well, none that we have found.' Moses ignored him but Nesbit cocked an ear. 'George Haggerty did not kill his wife Abigail or his son Malcolm. He couldn't have done it.'

To his mind the best way of getting Costello back was to prove her wrong and get DCI Mathieson and her team to prove that somebody else did kill Abigail and Malcolm. Then maybe Costello could get closure and move on. And then she might come back into the fold as it were. He could see how the lack of progress in the case might have frustrated his colleague. The killer had ghosted in and out the house, without leaving a trace. Or a trace was there because it had a right to be there. The Haggertys were not a social couple so the only 'other' DNA in the house was Abigail's sister, Valerie Abernethy, and she had stayed overnight only a few days before the killings. No fingerprints, no footprints but the blood spatter had left a clean zone where the killer had stood and that indicated they were slim, five feet ten or more. George was five seven.

It had also really annoyed Costello to learn that Dali Despande's proposal to pilot a new fast-track child protection service had been side-lined, again. Looking back, Anderson thought, maybe she hadn't been right since the Kissel case, that child being starved to death, neglected by a mother who didn't care, let down by a failing social work system. It had taken that little boy weeks to die. Costello had sat in the court and relived every minute of the harrowing abuse. Then Malcolm? Costello had in her head that Malcolm was a vulnerable child.

Then she had walked into that scene, a scene so awful, it was reported that the crime scene photographer on duty had been off work since with stress, unable to cope with what he had seen.

Still none of it was any of his business. He had to walk away and leave it to Mathieson and Bannon. He had his cold case rapes to work on. Mitchum had given him one more week before the file went back to the freezer.

ACC Mitchum had been very clear; Anderson's loyalty was to the force.

Not that there was any conflict of loyalty, Costello had not been in contact for twenty-one days.

The Monkey House Of Horror.

The tabloids hadn't been able to resist that.

Valerie Abernethy looked up at the familiar ivy-covered eaves, the two red chimneys, the big, stained-glass window all hidden from the road by the majestic monkey puzzle tree. Had it been a happy family home for her sister? The gutter press thought so. A happy family home that became a scene of slaughter.

Valerie took a deep breath, trying to calm the panic. They wanted her to walk round the room where her sister had breathed her last, shielding her son from the blade of a knife. She was aware of the investigative team hovering at the bottom of the gravel drive, pretending they were giving her a little moment to catch her private thoughts. She knew she was under scrutiny.

Well, they could stand there, out in the rain, a little longer. Valerie placed her hand on a petal of the stained-glass flower, a delicate stem with Mackintosh roses. The glass felt slightly warm to her touch, almost soft under her fingertips.

The front door was familiar and welcoming, painted claret to match the colours of the roses. The brass knocker that Malcolm used to polish managed to shine, even in this God-awful weather. The door was open. They wanted her to go in alone.

She had no idea when she was last here. Her memory had large gaps.

A lump caught her throat. This was too difficult. She tried lifting her foot to get her up the step, one stride and she'd be in the house. Nothing happened. Her leg was leaden, stuck to the red tiles. Valerie recognized that feeling, an old enemy returning.

She needed a vodka.

She closed her eyes and stepped up. She had to do this for Abigail. For Malcolm.

She was now stock-still, one foot up, one foot down and with her fingertips still resting on the glass window. There was movement behind her. Archie Walker was about to intervene and offer his assistance.

She needed to do this on her own.

Valerie turned her face up to the sky and took a deep breath. The raindrops spat at her with disgust, stinging the skin of her cheek. She didn't think it would be as hard as this.

Did she remember that night six weeks ago? Could she remember, vaguely, walking out the hospital? Standing in the light rain in Great Western Road, watching the traffic? She was probably looking for an off licence. Then there was a smell of perfume she could recall, something familiar she recognized from Abigail's house. Was that merely an association of ideas, her imagination filling in the blanks?

Another pause.

A rustle of impatience from the drive.

That would be the boss, a small fascist detective with hard flinty eyes. That cop was mistaken if she thought her pillar-box red lipstick distracted from the incipient Hitler moustache. Her junior officer, the big bearded bloke, kept a good four paces behind her. Like Prince Philip.

Fascist and Beardy, it was easier than remembering their names.

Valerie heard footfall behind her as the cops and Archie, here in his role as her godfather, not in his professional role as the chief fiscal, were walking up the gravel driveway. They only moved because it was too wet for them to hang around outside but it still felt like harassment.

Bugger them. She would do exactly what DI Costello had done on the day she had discovered the bodies. Valerie pulled away from the front door and walked briskly round the house to the back garden.

Now she turned to confront Fascist and Beardy, wishing then away. They were standing across the path, blocking her way out. Archie gave her an encouraging smile. The rainwater ran down his face, to be cast off as he nodded his head. They were getting soaked through. Even better, Fascist had a sour look on her face, her lippy was about to run.

Valerie took a deep breath and walked in, recognizing immediately the stink of the forensic cleaning team, a scent she knew well from her days as a fiscal. This no longer smelled like Abigail's house; these rooms were no longer infused with the aroma of roses, fresh coffee and George's aftershave. She walked through the pristine utility room, the kitchen – everything neatly tidied away – to the back of the hall where her boots touched carpet for the first time. This was where Costello had spotted the tiniest smear of blood on the wall, blood that somebody had attempted to clean.

Valerie wondered how easy that had been to wipe away; probably easier to erase it from the wall than to erase from the memory. Fascist crept up behind her, and coughed in irritation.

'Is there anything missing that you notice?' she asked in her snippy voice. 'We have a comprehensive list of the items that Mr Haggerty has removed and we have the crime scene photographs and . . .' That earned her an elbow in the ribs from Archie, now standing beside her. Nobody wanted to be reminded of that.

'Anything missing?' confirmed Valerie, thinking that her sister's smile was 'missing', the hugs from Malcolm were 'missing'. The house was a mausoleum.

'Anything?'

Valerie looked around, climbed the stairs to the half landing and *Primavera*, resplendent in coloured glass on the west-facing window. The view east was totally obliterated by the monkey puzzle tree. It was an easy escape route; this window, down to the roof of the porch, a short slither to the ground. It was reported Malcolm had tried to escape that way once after an argument with his father. This was actually an easy house to gain entry and exit without being observed; the monkey puzzle tree hid a lot. She turned to look down at her companions, then up through the balusters to the upper landing, with its expensive Persian rug on an expanse of oak flooring. And a plain magnolia wall. Valerie screwed her eyes up to concentrate on what she wasn't seeing.

'Well, there was a picture there, a pastel. I suppose George took that, he always liked it.'

'What was the picture? I don't think he has mentioned it.' Bannon checked his iPad.

'A painting, it was a painting. A rowing boat on a canal, under willows, weeping willows. How fitting is that?' She turned to the other three. 'Uncle Archie? Did you say there was music playing when you . . . found them?'

Archie nodded, teary. 'Yes, that kid's song, it was on repeat on the CD. It had been playing for hours. "The Clapping Song", the one w-where . . .'Archie stuttered. 'Where the monkey got choked and they all—'

Valerie stared at the gap on the wall. 'They all went to heaven in a little rowing boat.'

Kieran Cowan drove along the loch side, through the dark night and the streaming rain. The engine of Ludwig, his 1977 Volkswagen Camper, hummed along nicely as the windscreen wipers beat a regular tattoo on the glass. The left one squeaking at the end of its sweep, the right one responding a millisecond later with a resounding *thunk*. He had been intending to fix that, but after a fortnight of constant rain, he had got used to the noise. It provided an irregular backbeat to 'Life in the Fast Lane', which blasted out the old Clarion cassette player at full volume.

He was used to this road. He would be able to drive even if the wiper gave up the ghost and fell off completely, spinning over the top of the van and flying into the night sky. He had driven Ludwig to Ardnamurchan once with a cracked windscreen, sticking his head out the driver's window until he could pull over and punch the crazed glass out.

Cowan kept his eyes on the road, the narrow stretches where he had to slow, the wider stretches where he could put his foot down and the nasty bends where he needed to hug the rock wall in case he met a HGV over the white line.

The clock on the dash was saying it was half eight. He wasn't in a hurry per se; he was a little concerned about time. As long as it was dark.

The job needed to be done, sorted and over with.

He drove confidently now, one hand on the steering wheel and the other steadying the rucksack that rolled and yawed in the passenger seat. The camera had been borrowed from the university. He had signed it out on Friday night to be returned Monday morning. It was an expensive bit of kit, a Macro Scub 4 underwater video camera. It was fully charged and ready to go, safely tucked in the rucksack along with his flask of tomato soup and some sandwiches. He had no idea how long he was going to be here. As someone with a gift for stating the obvious once said, 'It took as long as it took.'

Cowan drummed his fingers on the steering wheel in time with 'Life In The Fast Lane' as he waited for a short procession of traffic to pass, and when the road was clear he put his foot down. Ludwig's air-cooled engine whirred in protest. He turned onto the road that hugged the North-West side of the loch and accelerated, cruising along, singing tunelessly with Glen or Don, as he checked the clock again. He was probably a little early. He could have stayed at his laptop and got a more of his essay done but he wanted to be there first and check out the lie of the land, get a good spot where he could stay hidden.

Covert breeds covert.

He pulled into the deserted car park of the Inveruglass visitor centre, putting his lights off first so as not to disturb anybody already there. The car park was not entirely empty, there was a Mini parked at the front, looking out over the water. Cowan gave it more than a passing glance, his heart thumping, in case this was who he was looking for. But the windows of the other car were steamed up. He judged it had been there for some time and it looked as though there was still somebody in it. Or it might be two heads in the driver's seat, a lovers' tryst, a quiet night out on the lochside.

But he was mindful there was somebody there and he wished that Ludwig did not have such a distinctive engine.

Tonight could be the night.

He drove Ludwig into the far corner of the second car park, beyond the café that led to the other exit road. Nobody driving into the main car park would see Ludwig; he would be safely obscured by the dark and by the screen afforded by the single line of trees. He switched the engine off, letting the camper roll forward, closer to the pathway that went up the hill to the viewing point. That was where he needed to be. He lifted his rucksack and climbed out into the driving rain, glancing over his shoulder to see if he could memorize the registration of the other car. But at this time of night, at this distance, he couldn't even make out the plate but the car was of those new fancy Minis with the doors at the back, like his granddad's old Morris Traveller. They had tried to recreate a classic. A car that had been built as cheap transport for the masses had been reinvented as a lifestyle choice of the upwardly mobile professional with deep pockets, no soul and even less imagination.

As Cowan closed the door, he patted Ludwig as if parting with a faithful old horse. He tugged his hood up, pulled the rucksack onto his back and set off through the dark, rainy night up to the viewpoint to find a place to hide.

Valerie lay on the bed in the hotel. The banality of her surroundings leeched every bit of vitality from her.

She had felt the pressure since visiting Abigail's house.

It had left her unsettled, more depressed, but there was some comfort in knowing that this was the last day of her life. The knowledge many of us think we would like to have, but very few are brave enough.

Imagine Abigail not realizing that this was the last time she would stack the dishwasher, Malcolm not thinking that this was the last time he would do his teeth, pull on his Star Wars pyjamas and argue about staying up for another half hour. If they had realized that, they might have spent their final moments doing something less mundane.

Like saying goodbye.

Valerie had spent most of the morning rolling on the floor, lying on the tiles in the bathroom, or being sick down the toilet. Then out to the house before a sneaky foray to the off licence for cheap vodka, the quick consumption of which totally erased any memory of the walk round the house. But tomorrow the empty bottles would be lying in the corner. Silent, but ever present in their condemnation of her.

Well, she wouldn't be here to be condemned.

She lay for a few minutes on top of the bed staring at the ceiling, gradually pulling together the information she needed to place herself in time and space. Judging from the lunatic screeching of revved-up enthusiasm she could hear from the room next door, it was Saturday evening. *X Factor.* Or *Strictly.* Something awful. Anything.

On the ceiling was the familiar smoke alarm, the water sprinkler.

The last day of her life. She had done her duty, she had gone round the house. The feeling was one of overwhelming relief, all was as it should be.

She had a gun.

And a bullet in the chamber.

She turned on her side, pulling the pillow over her head and stared at the bland beige hotel room wall, thinking about the cleaner who was going to open the door to her mess, walking in to the room pulling her Henry hoover behind her then looking up to see a woman with her skull blown apart.

The bullet would do a lot of damage. Valerie knew it wasn't like in the films where the head lay intact, a neat trickle of blood delicately running down a sculptured cheekbone to leave a crimson teardrop on the pristine white sheets. The eyes, each lash point perfect with the mascara, the pupils open and staring into the sunset. Ready for their close up.

No, it wasn't like that at all.

Her head would open up like a flower, blood and brains would spatter all over the room, behind the headboard, behind the curtains. Over the fire alarm. Not pretty.

The crime scene pictures of Balcarres Avenue had been burned onto her retinas. Her sister and her nephew, bloodied and torn flesh entangled. And Abigail, her arms round Malcolm, a final, desperate attempt to protect him.

She would have been fascinated by it if it hadn't been so personal. The whole room was a gaudy abstract of cream and crimson, matching the stained-glass rose on the door.

That was another memory that wasn't going to go away.

She felt the weight of the gun in her hand.

No. She had to time this right, so it wasn't the cleaner who discovered her body.

Archie Walker? Yes, she'd time it so Uncle Archie would find her.

He could explain it to red-lipped Fascist and Beardy dogsbody,

She sat back up, looking at herself as her face passed in the mirror. A haggard young woman stared back out at her, seeming to move slower than she herself moved. A pale face haunted by the loss of her family, the loss of her career. Her loss of self.

Getting up and walking across the floor, she noticed she still had her boots on.

She should pick up the empty bottles of vodka from the carpet.

Why bother? She'd be dead. Oblivion was better than another AA meeting where they looked down at her, because she had lived a dream life. She had had it all. Yet they would stare at her as if she was some stupid addict, like she was one of them.

She pulled the curtains over the window, blocking out the night sky as she tried to remember. Glimpses of being wet, walking down the street, her hand had been sore. She had stumbled against the wall at some point, remembering the stinging pain as she grazed the skin on her palm. She looked at it now, seeing the bloodied scrape, a dark scab starting to form. Was that yesterday? Or this morning? This afternoon?

She had no bloody idea. This was the way of her life. Flashes of this. Glimpses of that. Nothing that ever made any sense. It was like listening to a foreign language, recognizing words here and there but never enough to pull together a sentence, never mind enough sense for it to form a story.

Memory lapse.

And she had no memory of what she was doing the day her sister was murdered.

But she had visited the house. It was over, closed. She could end it all now.

Sitting down on the side of the bed she took her boots off. Nobody committed suicide with their boots on. She wanted to be comfortable, lie down, and not leave the duvet dirty.

Dirtier.

She lay down again. Relaxing. Life owed her nothing except this one thing – this little bit of peace and quiet, save the whipped-up hysteria being broadcast from next door. Picking up the gun, feeling the weight of it in her hand. It was far heavier than she had expected. It smelled of oil, it covered the skin of her hands in something foul.

She wanted her last thoughts to be of Abigail. Of Mary Jane. And of Malcolm. She wanted to remember them as they had been in life. Abigail with her prim, controlled smile. Mary Jane pouting for the camera as every teenager had done for the last twenty years. And Malcolm laughing, both hands holding onto his most prized possession: his Lego Millennium Falcon.

All gone.

Had they all gone to heaven in their little rowing boat?

And what had happened to the Lego Millennium Falcon? It hadn't been at the house; well, she hadn't seen it. She had bought it for Malcolm last Christmas. Good times.

She felt the tears fighting to escape her eyes, but she refused to cry. There was nothing to cry about, not now. She looked back at the water sprinkler and the smoke alarm. Then heard footfall, somebody walking along the hotel corridor passing her door. They walked quickly with the quiet jangle of a key. A car key most likely, as all the rooms in the hotel were card operated, so he, she presumed, was going out to the car park.

Then the footsteps paused. The jangling stopped. Valerie's eyes fixed on the corner of the room, at the door, willing it to open, or not open. It seemed a long time before the feet moved away, going back the way they came. He had forgotten something. She wondered what.

Valerie tightened her grip on the gun, allowed herself a weak smile. Was that going to be her last thought on this earth? What had that man forgotten that was so important he went back for it?

She'd wait until he went away.

She made herself comfortable on the pillow, thinking about pulling it round and using it as a silencer. But it would be better if they all heard. Then they might be careful about who opened the door, especially if her forgetful friend outside happened to recognize a gunshot when he heard one.

She lay back and closed her eyes. The muzzle was cold against her temple, it jiggled around a little, the tremor of her finger round the trigger, the weight of the gun itself was heavy and unstable, holding it made her wrist ache.

She ignored a guffaw of laughter from next door. She said goodbye to the water sprinkler and the smoke alarm.

Valerie Abernethy closed her eyes and pulled the trigger.

Valerie Abernethy heard a click.

Donnie McCaffrey sat in his Mini Clubman on the north-west bank of Loch Lomond, at Inveruglass, alone in his car, slowly steaming up the windows. He was parked right at the waterside, the most obvious place. During the day, even on a cold winter's day, this place was alive and buzzing, but now, on a dark evening, it took on the mystical aura of shape shifters and moving shadows; the subtle movement of the water deceiving the eye into seeing things it had not seen.

Or had it?

There could be anything up here, hiding away from lights and prying eyes. He looked around again, cursing himself for having a good imagination.

Inveruglass car park was hidden by high trees, shrubs, a small signpost on the main shore road pointing to a concealed entrance that led to the observation viewpoint. He had been here a few times with Isla and the boys. A family day out at the waterside, time for a paddle and an ice cream. But now, waiting, he looked around the car park with different eyes. An easy drive to Glasgow. And easy drive up north. An easy place to find. But why here? Once through the thick bank of trees, the narrow entrance opened up to allow access to the small vehicle car park, the café and the lower viewpoint that looked over the metal pontoons and the plinth with its brass map of the water and every one of the fifty-four islands.

He looked at it now through the eyes of a criminal, an obvious entrance and exit, with the smaller secondary route at the rear, accessed through the narrow line of trees, well hidden in this dense dark night.

When he was here before, he had climbed to the upper level of the viewing point with his eldest on his shoulders, sweating his way up to the large wooden sculpture, An Ceann Mor, with its seats and standing areas. He remembered the sign, hanging at an angle, from a single nail, that said barbeques not permitted. The wood underneath was charred to ebony cracks you could see the grass through.

That day the car park had been bustling; tourist coaches stopping for comfort breaks and photo opportunities, boat tours dropping off passengers on the pontoon, bikers meeting for coffee, kids eating ice cream, little old ladies resting their swollen ankles and drivers stretching their legs, but everybody stopped to take in the breathtakingly beautiful sight of the long view of the loch. His middle boy had eaten so much ice cream, he had been sick on the way home. Twice. The new car had been three weeks old. He pressed the button to drop the window a little at the memory of the smell.

But this evening, Inveruglass was as cold and deserted as a Soviet winter. At nine p.m. on the twenty-fifth of November there were no tourists enjoying the view, no lights casting a shadow over the dark and still water. There were no coaches sitting with idling engines, no caravans tucked away behind the trees. The hills were silent against the dark, tumbling sky, and the rain was pissing down as usual, battering on the roof of the Mini where Donnie was trying to listen to 'Stay' by David Bowie, with the melodic shapes of Earl Slick on guitar, sideman par excellence.

He was enjoying himself in an exciting kind of way. He knew he had been early, leaving more time than necessary for his journey up from Glasgow and he was appreciating the solitude and the music. He had been happy to leave Isla muttering about starting her Christmas shopping, sitting there in her PJs with the Argos catalogue open and a worryingly long spreadsheet printed off at the ready. She had got as far as her brother-in-law's yearly subscription for *What Camera* magazine when Donnie's mobile had bleeped. He had read the text and had been intrigued, and a little frisson of excitement had brightened up his Saturday night in front of the TV. Isla hadn't questioned it; she had merely looked up from the spreadsheet and asked, 'Are you going out to work?' then a quick glance at the clock. 'You had better wrap up. It's chucking down out there.'

He had nodded, kissed her on the cheek and left the warmth of the family home, shouting goodbye to the three kids playing quietly upstairs, then closed the door of his three-bedroomed semi and climbed into the Mini; a man with a mission.

McCaffrey looked around him. It was a lovely, lonely site at the north of the loch, deeply inhospitable in this bloody weather. Why here?

Costello would have her reasons.

He checked his phone again, then the clock on the Mini's dashboard. Ten minutes to go, he gave some thought to Christmas; all that cooking, all that potato peeling, Isla's dad.

With a bit of luck, he'd be working.

He was turning that around in his mind when he heard another vehicle, bigger than the small Fiat he was expecting. The air-cooled whirr of an old VW? The oblong shape of a camper was highlighted for a moment as it swung into the car park. Its headlights illuminated the trees and the shrubs that surrounded the café, the arc of brightness shone on the empty shelves and the seats upturned on the tables before being switched off. The vehicle drove behind the line of trees, moving from his sight. McCaffrey looked in the rear-view mirror with professional interest. Was this what he had been summoned to witness? He slid down in the driver's seat, watching as a figure emerged from the bushes, thin and swift, moved quickly, driven by the weather but not furtive. He walked like a young man, an impression added to by long slender legs and bulky jacket. He was holding something in front of him as he walked in plain sight round the windows of the café, into the darkness, then reappeared as an outline on the secluded path up to An Ceann Mor. Then he disappeared.

McCaffrey stayed in the Mini, watching out the rear-view mirror, then twisting in the seat to look through the rear-passenger and then the front-passenger window, but the figure had gone, swallowed by the trees and the darkness of the sky. It was bitter cold and as dark as the devil's armpit, as his mum used to say.

At least the rain was easing. The windows of the car steamed up again. He wished he hadn't had that last cup of coffee. He'd need to brace himself, get out and have a pee in the bushes. And he'd be better doing that before she appeared. He'd need to be quick before his willy froze.

He switched the CD off, wondering about the owner of the campervan. The driver had looked young so McCaffrey's mind turned to drugs and God knew they had enough problems with substance abuse around here and in Balloch and Alexandria. And there had been a spate of killings of the wallabies that inhabited some of the islands on the loch. A couple of weeks ago, the carcass of one poor beast had been spotted by a tour boat. It had been skinned and pegged out on a small patch of sandy beach, a bloodied pink mass for the entire world to see.

That had made the front page of the papers and the drug issue was right in the public eye, now that it was affecting the middle classes and the tourists. And that guy from the campervan had been carrying something. If he was one of the gang killing the wildlife then there would be a small boat ready for him somewhere. The waters of the loch were very dark now.

McCaffrey made a decision, his nagging bladder forgotten. No wallabies were going to be harmed on his watch. He got out the car, pulling up the zip of his jacket before winding the scarf round his neck. He dug his hands deep into his gloves and walked round the back of the Mini, ignoring the bite of the cold wind that scurried in across the water and the reminders from his bladder. It had stopped raining but the chill ate at his muscles. He felt as if he was wearing no clothes at all. He shivered, jogging across the path on to the soft grass and stared into the car park, seeing the distinctive outline of the two-tone Volkswagen camper. When he was a boy, these were the transport of vegetarian peace-loving hippies not animal-torturing psychopaths. He turned, cutting across the other car park to follow the path of the younger man, walking up to An Ceann Mor, the big wooden structure with its bench seats and central walkway was easily visible against the skyline.

Maybe if the wind had been quieter, he might have heard the small van pull into the car park, its headlights out, and the engine off so the vehicle rolled with the lie of the land. If McCaffrey had looked back to check his car, he might have seen the man get out the vehicle, dressed in black, black gloves, black hat pulled low. He might have seen the long slim blade as he too followed the path to up to An Ceann Mor.

Valerie had no idea where she was.

Something rough against her lips, her shoulder numb and her feet very cold, sticking out of her warm cocoon. It seemed she was bound in a cloud of cotton wool; soft and warm, but it bound her all the same. She tried, but couldn't move any of her limbs, or straighten up, or stretch out. She had no hope of getting up on her feet. Her head hurt. Her legs were burning, her thighs sticky with her own urine. And the room was reeking with the dull smell of faecal matter.

That was obvious at least. She had shat herself.

Opening her eyes, she looked across a green field that stretched forever, until it reached a piece of wooden fence, a flat solid white fence. As she allowed her eyes to focus, in the dark that wasn't really dark, she began to make sense of it all.

She had fallen on the floor, rolled off the bed taking her duvet with her. From the feel of it she had hit her head on the way down, probably off the small white bedside table and as she had lain there drunk, as her bladder and bowel had voided.

That wasn't a first.

And then the full horror of it. This was a hotel room, not her home.

Slowly she tried to unwind herself from the duvet, trying not to throw up and add to the mess of the bodily fluids. Another thought stuck her through the maze that passed for her intellect nowadays. If this was in a hotel room then house-keeping would be coming in sooner or later. They couldn't find her like this, in this awful state. Alcoholism is the most private of diseases. It hides in plain sight.

In the end, after about ten minutes of writhing and slow acrobatics, she freed herself and crawled across the carpet on all fours, leaving the duvet, soiled and wet, in a pile near the bottom of the bed.

She got to the door and, holding onto the handle, she pulled herself up on her knees and listened. There was a flash of a memory. Could she recall, vaguely, being here the night before, between the first and second bottle? Doing something like this at some time? She flicked over the plastic sign hanging from the doorknob. On the inside.

Do not disturb.

Not even sober enough to put the sign out.

Still not sober enough to have an accurate memory of it.

From last night or this morning? Or this evening? She opened the door as quickly as possible, peering down the corridor, to the right and to the left before she slid the sign out, the scab on the palm of her hand nipping as she slid it up against the wood to the handle.

She retreated inside the room and tucked herself in the corner of the carpet and the door. She closed her eyes and slid down a little more, her body folding onto the floor.

Her eyes were crusty and jaggy. She picked at her eyelashes with inaccurate fingers, missing the islands of scabs, poking herself in the eye a few times, making her blink. She could sense the solidity of the darkness outside the room now. It was very quiet, much later at night. Maybe midnight. Maybe not. Time was very elastic these days.

Closing her eyes again, she tried to stand, levering herself up between the door and the wall, and then she saw the bed, minus the duvet, with the expanse of rumpled white sheet with dark islands of staining, and in the middle, framed by wrinkles in the Egyptian cotton, lay a small black gun.

A gun.

And then, as she held onto the wall, she remembered.

She couldn't even kill herself properly.

She was a high-functioning alcoholic and had been for years. Her drinking never bothered her, it was life she couldn't really contend with. She had never suffered bad hangovers because she had barely ever sobered up. The constant top-ups gave her strength and kept that black dog from snapping at her too much, kept it from biting at her heels. She drank to be happy. Her drinking had brought her to this misery.

Why did she get a gun that didn't work? What was wrong with her that nothing, nothing ever went right?

She was too tired, and too sore to cry. What was the point? She picked up the gun and slid back down to the floor, her head thumping as she went. Crawling over the carpet, pushing the gun in front of her, she thought how bloody stupid it would be if the gun went off now and blew her leg off, or her arm off or half her face. Or if it went right through her brain, in the front and out the back, leaving her a dribbling incoherent vegetable, a bag on a drip in her arm putting nutrients in as the catheter took the metabolites out to fill another bag. She tapped it along a little more gently, slipped it into her suitcase using the zipped pocket at the side. Then she thought again, and stuck it into her handbag.

Her mobile phone was lying on the floor where she had flung it, so she slithered across the floor towards it. The black screen refused to swipe into life. She hadn't charged it up. Nobody had called her for weeks now, nobody except the police, and lawyers, and they weren't calling Valerie Abernethy the woman. They were calling Valerie Abernethy the victim. Or the suspect. No friends ever called her. No friends had called when Abigail had died. No friends had visited her in the hospital.

Alcoholics do not have friends. They use people so much that friendships wear away, slip away, here with the roses, and gone in the autumn.

It was winter now, the deep, deep winter.

TWO

Old Salty's Fish and Chip Emporium was busy, and very noisy. Adding to the usual chattering and cutlery commotion was the family at table eight, who were having some birthday Jenga-with-chips competition. The very attractive Australian waitress was judging and the rest of the restaurant were clapping and taking bets.

All except the four men sitting at table nine.

Four men on a table set for five.

They were subdued, three of them picking at their chips with their fingers, the eldest of the four using a fork. Failure has a bitter taste that no amount of cheesecake can sweeten; they ate as if their food was choking them, totally oblivious to the birthday celebrations in the next booth.

The four men; three detectives and a procurator fiscal. It was the first time they had met since the brutal murder of Abigail Haggerty and her son Malcolm six weeks before.

Not something anybody with a human soul should get over quickly.

They had an unspoken pact not to talk about it. That had lasted until the first lull in conversation, between the fish and chips being cleared away and the arrival of the cheesecake. They had exhausted the 'how are the kids doing?' conversation for Gordon Wyngate, and the 'how is Baby Moses doing?' conversation for Anderson.

Archie Walker related the story of walking round the house with Valerie and the missing picture and Lego model. At that point they all tried to avoid talking about Costello when she was the one thing they really did want to talk about; she was their thread of commonality.

It was a puzzle that consumed the detectives, eating away at their core. At the heart of the case was a strange coincidence, which was later revealed not to be so much of a coincidence at all. The Blue Neptune Case and the deaths at the Monkey House, as the tragedy of the Haggertys had become known, were 'intertwined, but legally separate cases' as the fiscal had put it. And the Haggerty case was under the eagle eye of DCI Diane Mathieson. Those sitting around the table, as part of the original team at the Blue Neptune, had been debriefed, welcomed, tolerated and then told in no uncertain terms to 'bugger off and to stop trying to be helpful', according to DI Bannon or 'stop bloody interfering', according to DCI Mathieson.

While they had no reason to meet, none of them had wanted to be the one to call off a date that had been pencilled into the diary for weeks. And they wanted to know about the problem. Costello's empty chair.

DCI Colin Anderson, the blonde detective in the jeans and casual shirt, had had very little to do with the case profession-ally, but he had a declared personal interest. This personal interest, the discovery of a daughter he never knew he had, automatically precluded him from any further professional connection. And he was becoming aware that it wasn't in his nature to accept that.

Archie Walker, the fiscal, looked to be his immaculately dressed self, but the constant drumming of his fingers, the frequent glances at his watch, betrayed him. He might have been trying to fool himself that all was OK in his world but he was having no luck fooling the three detectives round the table with him. His goddaughter was suspected of murdering her sister and her son. And she had no alibi. No memory. Only now was he discovering the issue of her alcoholism, mostly from reading his online newspapers.

Viktor Mulholland was watchful, keen to enhance his career here. This situation was a mess and he knew Diane Mathieson. He might hear something round this table that he could casu-ally mention to her. Indeed, she was already approaching him, not any of the others, for any information she needed. That might be a simple matter of rank, but Mulholland suspected something more political. Mathieson was a player and Mulholland hadn't quite come to a decision about which team to back. His present career trajectory was on shaky ground.

With Costello gone, and the increased likelihood of Anderson going, the solid peg he had pinned his entire career on was now looking very shoogly indeed. And Mathieson had a reputation as a two-faced wee bitch. Being a cop who investigated cops was bad enough, but her track record was worse than most. She was after Costello for harassment of George Haggerty. And that complaint was justified.

Mulholland didn't like being associated with Anderson's team, not now Complaints were sniffing around, but he didn't enjoy the thought of being exposed in a new team led by a woman with only her own ambition at heart, so he was watching both Anderson and Walker carefully. Both men seemed deep in thoughts that he would like to have access to.

However, Gordon Wyngate was happily eating his cheesecake, aware of the tensions round the table and easy in the knowledge that he would be the one who would unwittingly broach any forbidden subject. So he did. 'When's the trial starting?'

The silence fell like a rock through a cloud.

Wyngate wanted the ground to swallow him, Mulholland merely smiled.

'No date set yet,' said Walker calmly.

'Do you think—' Wyngate stopped as Mulholland accidently stabbed him in the thigh with his fork and interrupted with a question of his own.

'Is Braithwaite still blaming everybody else?'

'Yes, and he has Tomlinson defending. Well, I have heard.' Walker intertwined his fingers and placed his chin on the mound of knuckles.

'You have Valerie's testimony. She survived. You were out with her yesterday, she must be getting more . . .?' asked Anderson, the question had to be asked now.

'Sober? Do you mean will she be fit enough to appear as a coherent witness? Is that what you are asking?' Walker snapped. He was touchy on the subject of the darling goddaughter who had fallen from grace so spectacularly.

'No, that's not what I meant, not at all. I meant, can she stand up to that questioning.'

A roar of excitement went up at the Jenga table.

'She lost her niece, then her sister and her nephew.' The fiscal she'd keep in touch even if to tell me what a fair-weather friend I was, if in less polite terms.'

'You thought wrong.' Walker was still spikey.

'What I meant was,' Anderson picked his words carefully, ignoring another cheer from the Jenga table, 'none of us know where she is and she's not one to go anywhere quietly. This meal was planned for five. She was icily polite when she refused the invite. She asked after Moses, said she was glad he was doing well and that I was to keep the baby away from George Haggerty as that man killed his wife and his child. And I was never to forget that.'

'How many times does she need to be told!' snapped Walker. 'She just won't accept the fact that George Haggerty has a cast iron alibi for that morning. They were murdered between four and six; George had left at one and was on the A9. The fact he looked at Costello "funny" at Mary Jane's funeral does not make him a murderer.'

'She told me he looked right at her and clapped his hands,' said Wyngate.

'She told me the same thing,' agreed Mulholland. 'And the "Clapping Song" was on the CD, on repeat, when she walked in and found the bodies.'

'That's the song where they all go to heaven . . .'

'Yes, I know,' said Walker quietly, closing his eyes, summoning some patience. 'I was there, about four feet behind her. Please, can we let it go?'

The table fell quiet as another table burst out laughing at some witticism.

Anderson said, 'I did ask George about it. He's round my house quite a lot these days to see Moses, so we do chat. He says he has no idea what Costello's talking about. He recalls seeing her at the funeral, he might have looked at her. He might have been brushing his hands against each other to keep warm. It was a cold day; he had just come out the crematorium. I was standing right next to him and there was bloody Costello hiding behind a Victorian gravestone like a ferret-faced Goth stalking the dead.'

The image made them smile.

'George Haggerty might not have been everybody's idea of

a perfect husband but he had cared, in his own way. I have seen his distress at the loss of Mary Jane—' Anderson took a deep breath – 'his adopted daughter, and my real daughter. He has been generous to me in that grief while his wife and his son were murdered. He's devastated; he's on some serious medication. And—' Anderson looked at them all one by one – 'he is Moses' grandfather, if not by blood. I am, as the DNA has proved. George has been dignified over that as well. That child was taken from him with little more than a glance at a test tube.' He nodded. 'When the court made that interim judgement, he said "do whatever is best for the boy". And he meant it. I don't think that's the act of a guilty man.'

'Sounds innocent to me,' said Wyngate. As the father of two wee kids, he felt he could judge that.

'And I bet Costello said that was exactly how a guilty man would act,' argued Mulholland.

'How does she think an innocent man should react to the murder of everybody he had loved in his life? Given her past, she should know the answer to that one,' said Walker. 'And there is the small issue of a total lack of evidence. As well as an alibi that can't be broken.'

'You checked?' asked Anderson, surprised.

'Bloody right I did. You?'

'Of course I did. So did Mitchum. I trust that bastard Haggerty as far as—'

'I thought you just said—'

'I know what I said, but that's not what I feel. I know exactly what Costello is going on about. Yeah, I asked around about that alibi. He's watertight. Police Scotland are his alibi. He was caught speeding up the A9. Dad in care home in Port MacDuff, care home phones the house at 1.10 a.m. George leaves after a bit of an argument. He stops on the road and texts the missus, she calls back. That all maps out. The mobile phone is where it should be. And then, thirty minutes later, he gets stopped by the traffic police. But Costello is . . . Well, George Haggerty is an itch she can't reach to scratch.' Anderson opened his palms, grasping for the right phrase. 'She's obsessed by him.' He caught Walker's eye, a shared thought that neither of them voiced. What the hell was she up to?

The Jenga tower at the corner table of Old Salty's got higher, somebody was clapping their hands together in delight.

Clap Clap.

'Have you and George really bonded over Baby Moses?' asked Walker.

'Well, Moses has Down's Syndrome, he's three months old. His mother sold him, the broker rejected him, his mother was murdered and he was abandoned in a stranger's car. I think the wee guy needs all the family he can get. He's great.' His voice was full of pride.

It was obvious to the others that while Colin Anderson and George Haggerty had indeed bonded over their loss, their relationship would fracture the friendship of Anderson and Costello. It explained her absence from the table.

'You can understand Costello being bitter. I'm bitter. I've known Abigail all my life,' said Walker. 'She would have loved Moses, if she had ever been allowed to know she had a grandson.'

Same way I'd have loved my daughter if I had been allowed to know she existed, thought Anderson, *but we don't make the rules.*

Anderson recalled the crime scene photographs, Abigail's arms wound tight round her son's body, just as she would have protected her, his own daughter, Mary Jane. She would have felt the same about her grandson.

Mulholland waved a sticky finger in the fiscal's direction. 'You have known the Haggertys all your life, and you accept that George is innocent.'

'I accept his alibi,' corrected Walker, carefully.

'And Colin, you share a grandchild with the guy, you know him, and you think he's innocent. Why the hell does Costello think she knows better?'

'Bloody female intuition,' said Anderson dryly, 'seemingly that trumps small things like evidence and cast iron alibis.'

'Well, she'll have to toe the line when she finally deigns to return to work, when she gets on with cases she's actually paid to investigate, not go off on a whim of her own. Yeah, a few days back and we'll sort her out.' Mulholland gave Wyngate an exaggerated nod, and got one in return.

Colin Anderson put his hands on the table then took a sip of his pint. Something about his manner, his quietness, cast unease over the rest of the table. 'She's resigned.'

'Fuck!'

'She what?'

Anderson looked at Walker, and gave him a slight shake of the head. 'Sorry Archie, I didn't know if you knew. She resigned on Friday the tenth. She wound up Haggerty at Mary Jane's funeral on the Friday, then spent all weekend asking you, me and the Baby Jesus for help. Then she hangs about Haggerty's house and he files a complaint for harassment. She gets short shrift and resigns, not wanting to be hampered by the legal restrictions of Police Scotland.'

'Resigned? Really? Resigned and didn't tell me.' The fiscal's face was etched with disbelief, that slowly morphed into hurt.

'She didn't tell me either,' said Anderson, 'I was told "formally".'

'Bitch,' muttered Walker.

'Stupid bitch,' added Mulholland.

'Brave though, that takes some balls.' Wyngate raised his glass, they toasted her.

'To Costello's balls,' said Mulholland.

The mother of the family in the next booth turned to give them a dirty look. The chip tower of Jenga collapsed.

A tourist bus crawled past, part of a new Explore Scotland initiative; Glasgow at midnight, on a bitter cold November Sunday; the open-topped upper deck was empty apart from the two drunks leaning off the back of the bus singing a song about where to shove your granny. The downstairs of the double decker was steamed up. Anybody in there would see nothing but glazed lights and a dense smirr of rain, which was probably just as well.

'I do worry about Valerie, she wasn't exactly stable before the murders. Something I have only become aware of in hindsight.'

'She was married though, so there was a somebody once?'

'He left her because of her drink, I know that. Now. She was like a robot walking round the house on Balcarres Avenue, no tears, no emotion. It all seemed too much trouble for her. Talking about a picture that was missing, where was the Lego model she had built at Christmas? Was George going to sell the house?'

'You know murder transforms those it touches. Valerie's not immune because she's part of the judicial system, she has lost everybody,' argued Anderson.

'I don't even think she sees George now.' Walker glanced at his watch, 'I suppose I should go and visit her. She's staying at the Jury's.'

'Really? It's very nearly midnight.'

'Alcoholics don't sleep, recovering ones sleep even less. And she's in a hotel because she's skint. She sold her flat to try to buy a baby, remember.'

Archie Walker wasn't ready to sleep and he wanted to clear his head. It was only a twenty-minute walk from Byres Road to the hotel where Valerie had been living for the last three weeks. She'd be awake. Insomnia was one of the reasons she had reached for the bottle. He'd get there and phone her. If she answered, fair enough, if not he'd walk on to his own house which was another ten minutes along Great Western Road.

It was one of his conditions to get her to stop drinking. He would pop in with no advance warning, and she had better be sober. So far, for him, it was fifty fifty.

As he watched the steady rain, the glow of the traffic lights, he wondered about her memory lapses, and the nagging doubt at the back of his mind. Valerie was a fiscal, she had been a talented prosecutor in court, fierce when she was at the top of her game. Would she know how to commit a perfect murder?

Since the incident at the Blue Neptune, Abigail had said Valerie could stay at her house, but Valerie said she had not been there, or if she had, she couldn't recall it. If she had been there, she was drunk and nobody else left alive could bear witness to what had happened. Valerie had been in the house on the eleventh of October, three days before the murders. Her prints had a right to be there. And the perpetrator had taken their time in the house, they had known the house, known the victims.

And in Mathieson's view, a fiscal would be well placed to do that, but whoever had committed that atrocity, had a clear and precise thought process. Not the Valerie that he now knew, the one who crawled around the floor, too pissed to stand up.

He watched two young women, giggling as they got off the bus, deciding walking would be quicker than waiting on the late-night traffic through Queen Margaret Drive clearing. Their laughter made him think of how Valerie had been his favourite, the quiet thoughtful one. Abigail was the loving wee girl then, a normal happy child, mischievous and playful, a free spirit. She was fun to be around.

Anderson nudged him. 'Now we are on our own, tell me, do you think she did it?'

'Nope, she'd have been so pissed she wouldn't have cleaned up, it was a cool methodical mind committed that crime.'

'OK, does she share Costello's suspicions of her own brother-in-law?'

'Valerie is the one with no alibi, not George.'

'Answer the question Archie.'

'Yes, she does.'

'Come on, let's walk up to Oran Mor,' Anderson suggested; it was too cold to stand still. 'So what was Abigail like?'

'I was just thinking that. She was happy. A GP, bright. She was happy then Oscar, her first husband, was killed in an accident, boating, I think. Car? No, drowning. She ended up going to court to get him declared dead.'

'That takes ages, seven years?'

'Indeed. Mary Jane was about six or seven at the time he went missing.'

'They seem to be a very unlucky family,' said Anderson thoughtfully, standing at the kerb, waiting to cross Byres Road. 'But I do see Costello's point that no family can be that unlucky, which suggests it was nothing to do with a lack of luck.'

'Maybe that's not true, maybe in a roundabout kind of way everything is linked.'

'A butterfly flaps its wings in Columbia and the number twenty-seven bus gets diverted through Clydebank? That kind of thing? Come on, let's cross.' They both jogged across the road, cutting between the four lanes. 'It's not a small world when the fish swim in the same small circles. I still don't understand why Sally never told me she was pregnant. I'd have stood by her. I'd have wanted to know Mary Jane.'

'Maybe she didn't know the baby was yours. Or she did and didn't want you to know. She was with Braithwaite at the time and we know what a psycho he turned out to be. Maybe it was self-preservation.'

Despite the tragic ending to the situation, Anderson smiled. 'It was a drunken night in the park when her bloody boyfriend had buggered off elsewhere. So yeah, not proud of it, but we were young and, maybe not in love but in lust at least.'

'Well, there you go then, at least you are human.' Walker stopped to put a pound in the box of a homeless person. Anderson patted the Staffie cross that was snuggled under the blanket and gave him two of Nesbit's treats. They walked on. 'I've been thinking,' proclaimed Walker.

'Be careful,' cautioned Anderson. 'You're a lawyer, it's against your religion to think without getting paid by the hour.'

They walked on, up to Oran Mor, watching the remnants of the rain fall as orange and golden tears, catching the glare of the street lamps and the headlights of the traffic waiting at the Queen Margaret Drive junction.

Walker spoke with a sigh, 'I really do need to go and see Valerie, I'm feeling guilty. I think she's hiding from me. She thinks that she has let me down, again. Especially at the house. She could barely be bothered to put a comb through her hair, or wash her face.' He shook his head, being as perjink and neat as he was, this was a heinous offence. 'Maybe she became a lawyer for all the wrong reasons. Who can cope with months and months of working on child abuse cases when she was yearning for a child she couldn't have. I'm her godfather. I'm supposed to look after her spiritual welfare, so I buggered that up good and proper.'

'She buggered it up herself. At one point, Valerie was on a good career ladder if she was already in charge of a unit in Edinburgh. She was doing OK. At one point,' Anderson repeated.

'She was, at least until . . . until her marriage broke up, until she realized that she was going to have difficulty having kids. Then she began to drink. It was the pressure of the job, the pressure of going through every test in the book, with a husband that thought it was all too much bother. Grieg, her husband, had more of a *que sera sera* view on the subject. I'd like to think if I had a fiscal in my office with failed IVF behind her, I'd have the sensitivity to transfer her away from a child abuse unit. I saw her falling apart, I tried to intervene, talk to her boss to get her moved, but they wouldn't do it unless she asked, and rightly so . . . well, I thought that was a shit decision. It had to come from her, but she was far too proud to say that she couldn't cope.'

'She was very well thought of at her job, and she's still young. She'll get back to it, once all this calms down. She'll get back on track, just needs a bit of time, a bit of support to get off the sauce.'

'I don't think I can be bothered with her nonsense tonight.' He sighed. 'Is George really round your house a lot?'

'Too much for my liking,' answered Anderson truthfully. 'At times I like him, other times he gives me the creeps. He walks about my house, he drinks tea with my wife, he cuddles my grandchild; the child of a girl he adopted so I can't deny him that, can I? Mary Jane was in his life for twenty years. I never met the girl, and then I waltz in and take the only surviving relative George has and claim him as my own. By rights that child belongs to him.'

'You need to think practically, you have a house, a wife, a bank account that can support it all, George Haggerty is bereaved mess, he lives here and in Port MacDuff, two hundred and fifty miles apart. He shuttles back and forth. Not exactly stable. I think you are doing the right thing, I don't know that I could do it.'

They stopped at the corner outside Oran Mor, beside the bus stop, a couple of Jack Russell terriers crossed the road, their double lead tied to the handles of a bike with no lights ridden by a Chinese student. She nodded at them in acknowledgement for clearing the path for her. 'Yet a woman whose judgement we both trust believes this so much she has resigned from her job.' Anderson smirked. 'Mitchum said that she told him to take a running fuck?'

Walker smiled.

'Does she say much in the texts?'

'It's all very civilized.' He pulled out his phone. 'She never told me that she has resigned though. I guess she thought I would talk her out of it.'

'Do you know what she's up to?'

'Nope, but I presume she's after Haggerty.'

'Do you think she's going to do anything stupid?'

'Yes.'

'So do I.'

Wilma Patrick laid down her knitting and fumbled for the remote before that dreadful reality TV show started, the one where the 'stars', who had spent their youth at the best public schools in England, couldn't string a coherent sentence together. Wilma had retired for health reasons having taught primary pupils for over thirty years, nothing wrong with a bit of ABC and 123 before they started all that vertical learning and companion studies nonsense. She had taken her package before she said something she really meant during a meeting. She blamed Alastair of course. Being married to him always gave her a different perspective on life. And the lack of it.

The remote had slipped from the arm of the wheelchair and had disappeared under her ample buttocks. She wriggled around and poked under the cushion, before shaking out her knitting. The remote went flying across the floor. It spun round and spilled its batteries under the dog basket.

Hamish the Scottish terrier opened one eye, judged there was no food involved in this disruption and wasn't for moving, so Wilma wheeled over and turned the channels over on the Sky box, poking the button with her knitting needle. There was a new Scandi drama starting on Channel 4 that she wanted to see. She had perfected the art of reading subtitles and knitting a complicated Fair Isle pattern simultaneously.

She reversed herself back to the sofa. The programme was starting in less than five minutes so she'd wait until the first advert break before she shouted at Alastair to put the kettle on. He always spent a Sunday night doing his guitar homework, though why, she had no idea as he had a tin ear. He had to stop the singing lessons when he made Hamish howl, so he had taken up the guitar now. It was no more tuneful but it was

quieter. Wilma understood it was therapeutic for him to plunk
away.

The programme started and she settled back. A young girl,
in her early twenties, was walking through a field of corn in
the windblown rain. She had the obligatory Nordic jumper on,
her red hair and high cheekbones gave her the look of that
young constable Morna Taverner. The jumper and the actress
were being soaked by the rain, and would probably catch the
death of cold, thought Wilma. But, knowing these dramas, the
girl would be dead by the first advert break anyway. She knitted
on, with one eye on her needles and the growing tapestry of
colour spilling across her lap, the other on the screen. The girl
was running now, her arms pumping. There was no music,
only the sound of her ragged breathing, and heavy footfall.
She was running for her life, obviously. Wilma counted her
stitches, and listened to the rain battering on the living-room
window. The noise deafening, then quiet as the wind changed
direction. The weather had been foul all week. The Portree
– Port MacDuff ferry had been off more often than it had been
on. She turned her attention back to the television where a
man was now watching the running girl. She was still in a
cornfield. He was in a car, a Volvo of course, watching her
through the raindrops on the windscreen. The wipers went
back and forth, clearing both his and the viewer's vision of
her running away with her wet red hair straggling after her.
She was an elusive figure between the sweeps of the wipers.
Each time she reappeared she was further away. She might
just make it. The girl was obviously running away from him,
terror filled, not caring where she went, not looking back. She
did the obligatory stumble as she ran, her arms wind-milling
to stop her falling. There was music now, helping the drama
along. The man stayed in his car, watching as the camera angle
swept in so it was right on the girl's shoulders, as if the audi-
ence themselves were chasing her down.

Wilma liked that effect, she had to resist looking over her
own shoulder. She settled for a shiver.

The girl looked behind her, her small heart-shaped face
stared right into the camera. The corn parted, swallowing her.
She turned and ran straight into the arms of a big man.

There was a bang. Wilma jumped. Hamish woke up, ears alert. The screen went black and silent as the opening credits rolled and the image on the screen changed to a fat detective sitting in his office, swinging on his chair, drinking a cup of cold coffee. It always was in these dramas, they never had time to eat and they never went to the toilet. Wilma went back to her knitting, realizing she had dropped stitches, and tutting, unravelled it.

The scene with the detective moved on with no sound. The storm fell quiet allowing the sound of the guitar to float down, a few ragged chords, a song that got so far and then got stuck. It resumed but floundered at the same point. The detective on the TV started shouting down his telephone in Swedish. Or Danish. Or something. The music stopped again. This time it got far enough for her to recognize the song; one of Simon and Garfunkel's lesser known ones, the one about Emily. It wasn't one of her favourites, but Alastair had always had a fondness for it.

The scene on the TV returned to the cornfield. Filmed from a bird's-eye view that rose until the body of the girl appeared, lying in a small flattened area of corn, as if she was in a nest, comfortable and asleep. A few dots circled round her, policemen like vultures. The girl lay in the middle, a tiny spindle in a big spinning wheel.

Then the camera plummeted down like a hawk on its prey, crashing into the dead girl's eye, into the blackness and emptiness of one single pupil.

Wilma went back to her knitting as the investigation got underway. In forty-five minutes all would be well.

She heard another bang and looked up. Hamish growled at the front door, she thought she could hear the low rumble of a diesel engine. A car coming up the street, then doing a U-turn, there was a flash of headlamps and a squeal of brakes.

The music from the TV got louder, more dramatic.

She heard another bang, this time she knew it was the front door. She thought about ignoring it but that had been twice now. Maybe three times. She checked the clock; it was nearly midnight. Putting her knitting to one side, she wheeled to the window, pulling back her winter curtains by a fraction of an inch to look out into the bitter night. She saw a Land Rover bumped up on the pavement and flinched when she caught sight of the man, dressed in black, barely visible, standing in her front garden. He gestured that he wanted the front door opened. Now.

She let the curtain roll back, tensed in her chair, gripping the wheels, suddenly feeling like the girl running through the corn. Her husband got the awkward chord change and the tuneless song went on.

Jo and Walter had walked the same route every Sunday, around midnight, except when on holiday and the twelve weeks when Jo was off with her new hip. They sauntered mostly together, side by side, chatting and watchful. They looked like any other old couple, maybe a bit incongruous out on the streets of Glasgow in the witching hour; Walter with his thick anorak zipped up to his neck, a scarf tucked in to keep out the chill. Jo wore a navy blue coat that nearly reached her ankles but it did keep the cold away from her hips. Their faith and their uniform were both worn quietly, their belief more obvious in their compassion.

Over the years they knew who was on the street, who would be in what doorway, who might need feeding, who might kick-off, who was new and who might be saved in the Lord's eyes. Nobody was beyond redemption. But mostly, they sought out those who might be in need of a kind word and a bowl of soup, if not the loaves and fishes of the Lord himself. Though, they both hoped, that would come later.

Big Smout McLaughlin sometimes joined them. He was an enigma of Glasgow city centre. Tall, thin with chiselled features, articulate and well educated. They wondered, but never asked, why he chose to sleep in an alley at the back of the sheriff court. Sometimes he would come to the soup kitchen with a young one in tow, showing them there was always someplace to go if it got too scary out on the street. Smout McLaughlin had only ever stayed in the night shelter himself once in the twenty years he had been living rough and that was because of a vile chest infection. Jo reckoned he had somewhere to go when he needed, a safe haven tucked in his back pocket somewhere. To Jo, the maths were simple. People didn't last twenty years on the streets of Glasgow; pneumonia, sepsis or more recently TB would take their toll. All on the backdrop of the chilling wind and the damp, damp air that picked off the weak.

On this bitter November evening Jo and Walter were heading east from George Square. They had walked the concourse of Queen Street train station, had a word with the transport police. All was good. Next stop was Buchanan Street bus station, the first stop for many of the throwaways and runaways finding refuge in the cold, hard streets of Glasgow, or as their overnight stop on the way down south, to the colder, harder streets of London.

Walter adjusted the holdall he carried over his shoulder. It wasn't heavy, just bulky. It contained a couple of clean blankets and about ten pairs of warm woolly socks. They were heading, vaguely, for a young lad living in a box outside the side door of the bus station. Until recently he had been overnighting on the ground floor of the multi-storey. That was highly prized territory in the depth of the winter. Last week, the boy had his cardboard boxes back out on the street, tucked underneath the overhang of the station roof. And he had a bruised, bloodied face and a red socket where a front tooth used to be.

Tonight they found him, nestled into his fleece against his flattened cardboard. It was three degrees outside, the boy didn't have a pick on him. They woke him with a gentle prod, knowing that he would lash out before realizing they were handing him a blanket. Then they gave him the socks, Walter handing them over one at a time trying to make some kind of human, and humane contact, letting the eye connection last as long as possible.

The boy had woken up, flinching, his fist up ready but he didn't pull away. Seeing the socks, he immediately kicked off his dirty soaking trainers, one toe pushing off the heel of the other. Even in the stink of the human waste in the alley, Jo could smell the stench of the boy's feet from here. His toes were translucent grey, the skin round his toenails white and wrinkled, fisherwoman toes. There were deep dark tramlines where the seams of the socks had put pressure on the skin. She thought she could see the red puncture marks through the dirt in between the toes, but it was dark except for the overspill of lights from the concourse; maybe she was seeing what she expected to see. It wasn't her place to judge. The boy pulled on a pair of fresh socks, then placed his foot on the ground, soaking the dry sock, then pulled on his trainers.

Walter was talking to him, taking a good look, thinking that he was in his late teens at the most. Jo stood back, pretending to give him space and remain unthreatening, but really keeping clear of the dreadful smell. Walter's voice, friendly but not overly so, was telling the boy how close the soup kitchen was if he wanted something to eat, giving him rough, brief directions, before adding, if he couldn't manage they did have a van and could collect him. The boy was ignoring him, going anywhere meant giving up his space under the overhang. He was too busy stuffing the other two pairs of dry socks into his pockets and down his trousers. They were a prize and he didn't want them taken from him by unseen eyes watching from the dark.

Walter asked him if there was anything they could do for him. The boy looked blank. Even if he didn't speak a word of English, as increasingly was the case, there tended to be some response. Those in the clutches of heroin tended 'to roll' as Walter put it. Cocaine addicts rarely stayed still enough to fall asleep but this boy gave a resentful closed look before he went back to his business with the socks, pulling back the cardboard bed into the shelter of the overhanging roof. Two sheets had worked their way out from the wall a few inches and were swelling with the rain.

The look was more than Walter had got the last time, and an inch was better than a mile in the right direction. A look, then a word, then a smile, then he would be looking out for Jo and Walter to come walking along the street. Then a conversation and information. Then the boy was not that far from being saved from the streets and hopefully safe in the arms of Jesus.

Jo and Walter walked away, saying goodbye, wishing the boy would shout at them to come back but he didn't. Not this time.

Their next stop was usually The Heilandman's Umbrella, a section of Argyle Street under the raised tracks of the railway.

The shops and pubs were busy with shoppers during the day and clubbers out on the bevvy at night, and with the homeless and the lawless in the small hours. They preferred to get covered in pigeon shit rather than the constant Glasgow rain. Jo and Walter had turned into Buchannan Street precinct when Smout appeared, out of nowhere. This time he had a saxophone as well as his rucksack, obviously been doing some busking.

'How are you doing my friends, still doing the good work of the Lord?'

'While there remains good work to be done? Of course.'

It was a familiar exchange.

Their conversation was light hearted; Smout was not a lamb looking for a shepherd. He was more a collie looking after his flock.

He fell into stride with them both. 'There's a new one you might want to talk to, she's hanging about the bottom of the Buchanan Galleries. Been there all evening, confused. Older, definitely older and somebody has had a go at her already. And drunk, can't get a word out of her, you'll know by the smell, Eau De Thunderbird. See ya.' And he nodded, slapping Jo gently on her back, walking his jaunty walk into the darkness of Dundas Lane where he melted to invisibility, the smirr of rain swallowing him.

Walter consulted his watch and looked up as the rain started coming down in stair rods, jagged spears of orange in the streetlight, a night bus crawled its way round Nelson Mandela place, windows steamed up, engine groaning slightly.

'Shall we?' asked Walter.

Jo nodded. There was only one thing more vulnerable than the young on the streets of a big city. The elderly.

Ten minutes later Jo and Walter found the woman huddled into the corner of the steps of the concert hall. Her dark blue jacket had the hood up over her head and pulled tight round her face in an attempt to keep the world out. It was Jo who approached this time, even from a distance she could smell the alcohol but as she got closer she could see the blood on the side of her cheek, dried in a leaf-like pattern. The woman looked up, then when she saw Jo looking at her hands, she looked down at them also.

Jo approached as if she was a frightened animal. It could be
a mental health issue, she needed to be careful. Human bites
could be very dangerous. She knew that. But the older woman
stayed calm, staring at some point lying in the middle distance.

Jo tried a few opening lines: 'Would you like a blanket?
Something to eat? A bed for the night? Someone to talk to?'

There was no response at all. But she didn't react adversely
and Jo placed her hand on the woman's shoulder. Soaking
wet. That jacket was giving her no protection from the rain.
Jo turned and shrugged to Walter who pulled out his mobile
phone and called the community police as Jo got a blanket
from the bag and placed it round the woman's shoulders. The
woman, maybe not so old now, had looked up, vague recogni-
tion in her eyes as she reached out, her bony fingers moving
in the air, edging their way to the badge and the black
epaulettes on Jo's uniform.

And with a trembling finger, she pointed.

Wilma sat at the doorway, the warm living room behind her;
the hall had taken on the chill of the November air. She had
called for Alastair but he hadn't heard. She opened the door.

There were three of them, all dressed alike. One nodded to
her and invited himself in.

He said one word. 'Tonka?'

Another stood back watching the street, one hand holding
a large torch, the other deep in his parka pocket. The man in
the doorway pressed closer, his hands crossed in front of him,
peering over her shoulders up the stairs, then followed his
colleague up, giving her a nod in passing.

Twenty years of peace and quiet, away from the madness,
and here they were knocking on her door at midnight. She'd
had her mouth open ready to protest, to ask them who they
were, exactly. But she had known, known from the minute
she saw them. No point in asking these men for I.D., that was
the last thing they would have given.

She tried to tell them there was nobody living here of that
name, no Tonka. It was a forlorn feeble attempt, her words
spoken to their backs as they went up her stairs, silent muddy
boots on her lovely new stair carpet. She could have wept.

They knew who they wanted, and they knew he was here. Another two men came inside and closed the door, dwarfing her and the cottage in their bulky dark blue and black jackets. Small men, in their thirties she guessed, young enough to be her boys. Hard faces, wide shoulders, alert and light on their heavy feet.

'Evening missus. Sit quiet and we'll be out of here double quick.'

Glaswegian accent. They usually were these people; Glaswegians were violent, any excuse. The guitar fell silent on a protesting chord. She waited, staring up the stairs.

Wilma had known that this day would come, shattering life's illusion like glass. It was a relief. There was nothing like waiting for that knock that never came. She kept to one side, her chair against the living-room door, but never taking her eyes off the top of the stairs where she could see a sliver of the man's body through the spindles of the bannister as he spoke softly, a quiet monologue. She heard Hamish whimper on the other side of the living-room door as if he also knew. She was still watching as the men came back down the stairs, moving at speed. They both nodded to Wilma as they passed, avoiding her eyes and they went straight out the door, leaving Wilma, in her chair, impotent in the possession of her own house. She watched them disappear into the black night, the dark wind swallowing them. She didn't hear the doors of the Land Rover open or close. Just the gentle pit pat of her husband coming down the stairs, carrying what he called his ready pack from the top of the wardrobe. He took his boots from under the stair, his jacket and his scarf from the hall stand. He didn't say a word to her or look in her direction in case he read it in her eyes.

Don't.

She looked into the ebony night, her eyes catching the twitch of the curtains across the lane as the neighbours had a quick look. She sat there alone and stunned as the Land Rover tail lights retreated and then vanished from her view as the vehicle turned the corner, hearing the engine accelerate hard, then there was nothing but the rattle of the rain and the howl of the wind.

* * *

The woman had said nothing on her way to the hospital, sitting in the back of the police car with ease and a degree of comfort, as if the journey did not faze her or she had absolutely no understanding of what was going on. The two cops who had picked her up, Turner and Whitely, had tried a few opening gambits about the weather and how it was far too cold to be sitting on a stone step at this time of year.

Silence.

Trying for a bit of chit chat, Turner asked her if she was hungry because they were passing ASDA and they could pop in for steak bake. Much to their disappointment she remained quiet, so they drove on.

She looked out the window, watching the nightlife of Glasgow float past; through the Clyde Tunnel, her eyes became wild and frightened. The blood was still steadily dripping from her head. Every so often she would fist it away, then rub the blood onto her anorak. Then look at the anorak as if she had never seen it before in her life.

At the desk in Accident and Emergency, Turner gave the details of where they had found her, and that they had no identification. He pointed to the blood on the side and the back of her head and to the overpowering stink of alcohol, both he felt being relevant to her story. He confirmed, in response to the receptionist's questioning eyebrow, that as yet there had been no reports of any missing person in the system who resembled this woman, and repeated that she had no ID on her, but they had only checked her outer pockets.

'I'll leave it to you lot to get her undressed and have a more thorough look. She's still bleeding.'

'No phone? No credit cards?' asked the receptionist, battering at the keyboard while her eyes flicked between Turner and the blonde woman. 'She OK?'

'Head wound,' Turner confirmed needlessly, then added that the patient was perfectly compliant, and seemed fully conscious. But wasn't talking.

'Can she walk OK?' The receptionist nodded towards the doors to the treatment area. 'Or do you want a chair?'

'She's a bit unsteady but she'll get through there. We'll stay until she gets sorted out. Is your coffee machine still on the blink?'

The receptionist pulled a sheet of A4 out the printer. 'Take that through with you and if you smile very, very sweetly, some nice nurse might stick the kettle on for you.' She gave them a huge grin that took sarcasm to an Olympic level. 'Make sure you've signed all your paperwork before you go. All of it, mind. And can you take that through with you,' and she opened the glass partition to shove a huge file into his hand. 'Dr Russell is wanting it. Well, somebody is.' The glass partition fell shut.

The two cops waited for the receptionist to press the green button and the door to the treatment area clicked open.

'Oh, hello you two. Three.' The nurse, her uniform straining to contain her ample figure, turned to the woman who was standing between the two cops like a young child, slightly nervous and waiting to be told what to do. The nurse looked at the slow trickle of blood meandering down the woman's forehead. 'Come on, sweetheart, I'm Hannah, let's get you through and find out what's been going on.' She placed a cupped hand under the elbow of the woman, easing her through the second set of double doors to the receiving and assessment unit. The woman paused for a moment and turned, as if reluctant to leave the two policemen behind.

'It's OK,' said Turner, 'go with Hannah, she will look after you. And while you are in there, we'll get a wee cup of tea.' Turner thought he saw a flicker of a smile in the woman's face.

'You know, pet,' said the nurse, 'they'll be lucky, getting a cuppa in here. Now you come with me, you'll be fine.' And they both were consumed by the blue curtains of an empty cubicle.

'What do you think?' Whitely asked. 'Domestic?'

'Could be. She stinks of booze. She could have fallen and hit her head and got concussion. She's developing that panda-eyed thing, so she's bleeding somewhere. Might be nothing in it for us but it's bloody freezing out there and nice and cosy in here so don't be so quick to get going.'

Whitely sat down beside him. 'Do you think we should see it through to the bitter end?'

'Oh yes. She's had head trauma.' Turner stood up to retrieve his notebook from his jacket and sat down, got comfy and started to write it up. Despite his levity, it troubled him a little. The woman was confused, non-vocal and had a nasty head wound that, weirdly, looked clean. Had she already received medical attention? Had she gone voluntarily? Had she had the wound cleaned and then a deeper bleed, some unseen damage now leaking into her brain that was causing a slow reduction in function? He had been a beat copper for twenty years and had seen everything, been bitten, spat at, punched, nearly stabbed a few times. Compliance like that was odd. She was quite at home in the police car, she smelled of alcohol but her eyes were straight and seemed to focus OK. And, apart from the blood, she was clean, well dressed; some attempt had been made to brush her hair, so most likely somebody somewhere was missing her. He radioed back to the station checking that no more reports had come up on the missing persons, reading out his initial description: sixty-year old female, blonde, grey-eyed, slim, five four . . . But that was all he knew.

The station checked the log, the number of people who went missing each day was incredible. The percentage who disappeared was growing as well, if people wanted to go, they would go.

They had one report that might fit. A Peter Gibson of Lochmaben Road in Crookston had phoned in to say that he had spotted a woman sitting on one of the benches at the perimeter of the small park known locally as the Tubs. She was wearing grey trousers, a long black jacket, white blouse. He guessed she was about sixty. Gibson had approached her, thinking that her clothes were not warm enough for this time of year and that she must be disturbed. Or drunk. Or drugged. Gibson had seen the blood on the white of her blouse and called 999. When the cops got there, she had run off.

Turner read the description again. Right age, wrong clothes. Not their woman.

THREE

Monday, 27th of November

Alastair Patrick did not say much to the three men. They said nothing to him; he was a package for delivery. A few curt words passed between them. Tonka cleared his dry throat.

How far?

A few klicks.

Where?

You'll see.

They were following orders. They didn't know any more than they were saying. They were being polite and they didn't have to be. They were tooled. Alastair Patrick had noticed the guns in the quick dash from the front door of his house to the vehicle. It was important to notice these things, the sort of things that made only stupid men argue. Even in the noise of the wind, he had clocked the thrum of the 2.5 diesel engine; he'd been struck by the dull reflection of the street lamp from the resin composite shell of the vehicle. He saw the protection over the front grille and the lights, the lack of number plate. Christ, it even had a snorkel.

A snorkel.

He almost smirked as he climbed in. Boys and toys.

It was black beyond dark once the vehicle pulled out of the street. Rain poured down making visibility difficult even in the bright glare of the Land Rover's headlights, the rapid thumping of the wipers on full throttle filled the vehicle. Once out of Port MacDuff, they were winding their way along the single track road to Applecross, the driver switched on the roof-mounted spotlights to aid visibility. He drove quickly, skilfully. His position was relaxed and comfortable, not leaning forward to peer through the windscreen. The demister set on screen roaring loudly, the Landie banging and heaving like a boat.

This guy, the Glaswegian, was a professional. He knew exactly where he was going. He drove with confidence as if he had driven this road before, many times in darkness.

Patrick knew they were skirting the coast, even with the blacked-out windows in the back of the Landie. As the vehicle swung round, he could see the sea out the front window, the sweeping beam of the Rua Reidh lighthouse between the swish thump of the windscreen wipers. He began to have suspicions as to where they might be going, and why, but he tried to dismiss the thought. Surely not even these three, the Glaswegian and his two gorillas, would be that stupid.

Patrick felt a tremor of controlled fear run down his spine, images darting across his eyes, ball bearings flashing past in strobing light. A sledgehammer thumped in his heart at the intense memory of his mate Zorba, caught between the crags, screaming at his missing legs. Patrick blinked the image away, wiping his lips with the back of a gloved hand, removing a telltale smir of nervous sweat. Never show them that you are scared, once they know that, they own you. Some things don't change. Even now, helpless, he couldn't help planning how to take them. Some things, like old habits, die hard. And he believed that he also, would die hard.

He hoped it wasn't tonight.

He looked ahead, examining the back of the men's heads. Identical thick necks, short haircuts, the dark blue and black jackets invisible in the hours of darkness, the pattern varied to disturb any outlines. Their woollen hats were pulled down, the rim tucked up. Rolled out, their faces would be covered, save for two round holes at the eyes.

As they turned inland, Patrick tried to work out what to do as the windscreen wipers battered across the toughened glass. He wondered how the Glaswegian could see where he was going, even with all the extra light that dazzled on the tarmac in front of them making spotlights dance on the road as rocks swerved, slid past and then vanished to darkness. The Landie occasionally bumping slightly as it impacted something unseen.

He looked at his watch. It was half one. Zero One Thirty Hours.

Instinct, training, made Patrick strap himself in tighter as the vehicle really began to bounce around with more force, the driver taking out the corners of the twisty road, moving faster than was safe. He tried to take in as many details as possible. He was sure he didn't know any of the three men. The Glaswegian, his Gorillas, the brains and the brawn, but he knew the type.

Holding on to his seatbelt with both gloved hands, he looked round the vehicle: military, operational. He swore as it veered a sharp right, he heard the gears grind in protest but the driver didn't let up as the incline suddenly steepened. Patrick gripped the seat belt tighter, trying to secure himself in the seat, his boots bracing against the brackets. It got darker outside as if the headlights had died and he could only see the small lines of prickly skin between the hat and the collar of the gorilla in front of him. He closed his eyes, wrapping himself in his waxed anorak, a thick woollen scarf, knitted by Wilma, pulled tight round his Rohan hat and his hill walking boots. He had put on his warmest Thermawear jumper.

He was freezing.

The Land Rover jolted again, a teeth-juddering, bone-shattering jar.

'You have got to be joking,' he muttered, looking right at the back of the head of the Gorilla, as the vehicle tackled a hairpin bend. The Glaswegian's black-gloved hands on the steering wheel pulled to the right, letting it slip through to return to neutral. Calm. Controlled. Then Patrick realized he recognized the road; he thought he caught another glimpse of the shimmer of water to his left; the Inner Sound, the deepest territorial water in the UK. He thanked a God he didn't believe in, that the Landie had turned further inland. There was a flash of domestic light ahead, engine screaming as it tackled another ascent. The driver had taken a left turn out of Applecross. And that could only mean one thing.

They were going up the Bealach Na Ba.

'No. No way. Are you ripping the pish?'

'Nobody's laughing,' growled the Glaswegian, moving the armour-plated Landie, an all-terrain vehicle, as if it was a Ford Focus.

There was no point in asking why, they wouldn't tell him, mostly because their orders only took them so far. After that, something else? Someone else? But the driver knew exactly where he was going, Patrick just wished he was in a bit less of a hurry.

He fell back into his own silence, memories coming back, how easy it had been to slip back in harness. Even after all this time to drop into automatic mode. 'Claymore'. His activation code had unlocked the door to the ghost world, a path to slip back into this way of life, a life of hard men and hard choices. No compromise. He decided to stop being brave, he was no longer a young man. He had left those days far behind him.

Or so he thought.

He shut his eyes and waited for it all to stop.

The Landie side shifted with the strength of the wind. They must be high up now, nearing the peak. This vehicle weighed tons yet it was being blown about like a toy car, buffeted by the wind as if the hills were pushing them away, they were not welcome here. Only a mad man would be up here at midnight driving around at altitude, in the dark, in fifty-mile-an-hour winds and driving rain.

He concentrated on the back of the heads of the two silent men in front, as they bobbled and lolled as the vehicle bumped and bounced. He was in the company of mad men.

It took one to know one.

It was past one in the morning when Colin Anderson let himself into his own house, the big house up on the terrace. He had left his own car in town, too drunk to drive back, so he immediately noticed the white Volvo parked in his space at the kerb. George Haggerty's car. Here to see his grandson.

Anderson closed the front door quietly behind him and let out a long slow breath. This was a difficult situation, and one that Anderson, while sympathetic, was getting more than a little fed up with. He slipped off his jacket and hung it up on the stand. Nesbit came running from the direction of the kitchen, looking innocent of any charges of fraternizing with the enemy. Anderson bent down and patted the velveteen fur of the dog's head as Nesbit leaned against his leg and twirled round and round, looking hungry. Anderson ignored him. It was an old ploy.

Anderson was sorely tempted to creep upstairs and go straight to bed, but that might be construed by his family as weak, or rude. And there was plenty of chatter coming from the kitchen, so somebody was up. He followed the noise and the dog's wagging tail, gritting his teeth slightly. The dimmer lights were on, the room was illuminated by a gentle amber glow more suggestive of a high-end café. His daughter Claire, and her friend Paige, were sitting round the table with George Haggerty, in between them was Moses, fast asleep in his basket on the kitchen table, snoring gently.

The first thing Anderson saw as he entered the room was George's little finger clutched in the baby's tiny, chubby hand. It was difficult to pull his eyes away from his grandson. If he had been slightly drunk when out with Archie, gently floating on a little sea of beer, he was grounded now.

'Hello. Do you three know what time it is?' Anderson said, consciously keeping his voice friendly.

'George popped in to see Moses, and to collect his drawing.' Claire waved a wine glass that seemed half empty of a full-bodied red, towards the parcel. Colin looked at it, then her. She was too relaxed to notice the dangerous glint in his eye, the one she called his 'look', the one that said *wait until we get home young lady*. He noticed the remains of Doritos, olives, bits and bobs of dips on saucers. Paige had a glass full of wine, the empty bottle beside her. Her peroxide hair was buzz cut, emphasizing the narrow snaky eyes that normally glowered at Anderson with suspicion and something that bordered on loath-ing. Now she was almost smouldering at him through her false eyelashes. Anderson ignored her, as he was trying to ignore that uncomfortable feeling he had about Haggerty sitting in his kitchen, pouring alcohol down the throats of two seventeen-year-olds. And then he felt guilty, as Haggerty stretched out an arm and shook him warmly by the hand. The man had lost Mary Jane, a young woman he had brought up as his daughter from the age of seven to twenty four, so maybe this round-the-table girlie chat was usual for him. Although, should the girls not be in their bed, or studying? Anything but drinking. Maybe he was old fashioned.

'Sorry, Colin. Once again I have interrupted.' George Haggerty, contrition glowing from his deep brown eyes, shrugged. 'I was about to go back up north to see Dad but I haven't heard anything and wondered if you knew of any developments. Anything at all, about Abigail . . .'

A huge tug on his heartstrings, then Claire joined in.

'Yeah Dad,' said Claire, her words slurring slightly. 'About Abigail? Surely they must have some news.'

'They are telling me nothing. And they will tell me nothing. I have a personal link to the case. Him.' He pointed to Moses.

'The case. The murder of my wife and child. The case?' George Haggerty ran his fingers down Moses' chubby cheek.

Anderson wanted to tell him to leave the baby alone. 'And that's why it's not allowed. If I don't think of it as "a case" and a job to be done, it would become personal and that can lead to mistakes.' Like Costello, he nearly added, then remembered who he was taking to, a man Costello believed responsible for the murders. He wished she was here now, smashing a wine glass across the table and stabbing him in the throat with it. At least then it would be over with. She would have the courage of her belief, not constrained by legality, decency and a lack of self-courage the way he was.

Anderson was aware that he smelled of drink so he walked round the table and switched on the kettle, feeling absurdly guilty. The man was innocent. He himself had been out socializing when George's wife and child had been killed and they had no idea who had done it, Police Scotland seemed to be doing nothing. He was aware of Claire's eyes watching him, wanting him to come up with something to comfort the man.

'Claire, have you not got uni tomorrow?'

'That's a polite way of telling me that I have to get up in the morning. Bloody hell, Dad!' She stood up, swaying slightly. 'And Paige's staying the night, if that's OK.'

Yeah, turn the house into a hotel why don't you? 'Why would it not be OK? There's plenty of room. And it's very late.'

Paige stood up as well, taking the last Dorito from a plate and slowly placing it on her tongue, seductively.

'You'll both want paracetamol and black coffee in the morning,' said Anderson, holding the kitchen door open, ushering them through.

George gave them both a smile, as they retreated to the hall. 'That Paige is worth the watching.'

'Indeed. She didn't have the best start in life so she's here getting some stability, if you can call this madhouse stable. You do what you can.' He watched as George closed his eyes, biting his lip a little.

'Nice thought, nice to try and make a difference.'

Anderson needed to be careful here. He kept reminding himself that this man had lost his wife and his child, and tried to wish him well. But somehow, he just couldn't empathize without immediately feeling a churning anger that it might have been him who killed them.

'Do you want a coffee? I'm having one,' said Anderson.

George shook his head, his arms out. 'No, no, I didn't want to interfere with your night. I popped in to see Moses and the girls invited me in. I had brought you a nice Rioja. They have drunk it. And I had a game of Zombie Gunship with Peter. He beat me, he absolutely wasted me.'

Anderson made an empathetic noise as if he knew what Haggerty was talking about, trying to hide the increasing unease that Mr George Haggerty was becoming so familiar with his own children. And a rage of jealousy that Peter had never, ever, asked his dad to play Zombie Gunship with him.

'Yet again I have abused your hospitality, but I did want to know if you had heard anything.' He sat back down, waiting and cautious, keen for any details. 'In case you didn't want to say in front of the girls.'

'I'm sorry, George, but honestly, you probably know more than me. DCI Mathieson is good. She will be working away but keeping it from public attention. The exact time of death is causing problems. The pathologist thinks very early in the morning, you know, around six a.m., so why were they both dressed. They should have been in their night clothes.'

George nodded. 'They asked me about that. They were

dressed when I left the house. That pathologist told me they had to reposition the bodies at the mortuary so they could line up the wounds; some blows from that knife had gone through both bodies . . .'

Anderson was sure O'Hare had said nothing of the sort. 'Mathieson wants to trace the CCTV, try and get a vehicle check. There's a lot about the case that doesn't make sense.'

'They keep asking me if Abigail had another man in her life. She didn't, just so you know.' He turned to look at Moses, running his fingertip up and down the baby's chubby cheek.

Anderson wanted to ask him not to do that, but had no reason to, apart from that vague dislike. He had no reason for that either.

George turned and looked up, as if he had read Anderson's mind. 'I hope you don't mind me being here.'

'Well,' Anderson struggled to be honest, 'the circumstances are a little weird.'

'I like to talk to Claire; she is so very like Mary Jane.'

'Well, they were half-sisters,' said Anderson mildly.

George was staring at the door, watching the space where Claire had left the room. 'Claire has got such brains, concentration, focus. She's so talented. Have you seen this picture of Moses?' He patted the unwrapped package beside him, smiling.

'She gets that from her mum,' muttered Anderson, pouring in the boiling water to the coffee.

'They have the same gestures and the same . . .' Haggerty paused, a wry smile played around his lips.

'Attitude?' offered Anderson.

'Well maybe, in your daughter, it's a well thought out . . .'

'They were both my daughters,' corrected Anderson, then softened it with, 'but I know what you mean, something in that DNA that you cannot deny. Claire is an artist, Mary Jane was a singer.'

'Mary Jane *thought* she was a singer, that's not the same thing. She couldn't sing, no talent at all, but wouldn't be told. What a disservice we do our youth by letting them believe that everybody is owed their fifteen minutes of fame. And Mary Jane was nowhere near as intelligent or as instantly likeable as your Claire. This portrait of Moses shows a maturity beyond her years.'

Stay away from my children. Anderson pulled out a chair and sat down. 'Claire has been through a lot, far more than somebody of that age should be, but I'd like to think that she regards Brenda and I as constants in her life. No matter what she does, we will always be here. Mary Jane might have felt rejected by her birth mother, then her adopted Dad died, and then she was rejected again, maybe that coloured her whole life. If she knew it could be as precarious as that, why shouldn't she go and try to achieve what she wanted? I'm sure you didn't want to dash her dreams.'

'And then she dashes every dream she had by getting herself pregnant. And not a word to her mother or me.' George's eyes narrowed, as if not being told was the bigger issue.

'You didn't know?'

'Not until . . . no, I didn't. I do wonder if Abigail knew though. But she would have told me.' He placed his hands behind his neck. 'Mary Jane was twenty-four, she should have been able to cope with it on her own. I suppose she was drawn to having the baby adopted, as she herself had been.'

Anderson did not know how much George knew. Mary Jane was not having her child adopted; she had sold it just as her own mother had sold her. Mary Jane had sold her baby to a couple who had really wanted a child, just as, twenty-four years before, Anderson's old girlfriend Sally had got pregnant with Mary Jane, not told him and sold their baby to Abigail and Oscar Duguid. Nobody knew who Mary Jane's baby had been destined for as Moses had been born Downs Syndrome and had been deemed not fit for purpose.

And that made Colin Anderson very angry.

He presumed that there was a strange kind of karmic synergy in that. Did George really not know that; had Abigail kept the pregnancy secret from him? That would have rattled a control freak like him. Anderson sipped his coffee wondering how hurt he would be if Claire kept something like that from him. But she never would. Or would she?

No.

Anderson looked at the man sitting at his kitchen table,

drinking his coffee, talking about his daughter and his grandson. He could see how easy it would be to paint him as prime suspect, as Costello had done. His mouth opened before his brain could catch it.

'Did you report DI Costello for harassment?'

George had not expected the question. He had thought they were having a friendly father to father talk, not cop to witness, or cop to suspect. His dark brown hair fell over his forehead, giving him the appearance of a guilty schoolboy. His eyes darted around, he was thinking too long to answer truthfully. 'I think I did, I didn't mean to. I was sort of saying to somebody, one of your colleagues, that Costello was parking outside my house, watching me, when I had already been spoken to, my statement had been taken, my alibi confirmed.' He raised his finger to Anderson making his point. 'I had been cleared. Costello was annoying me for no real reason. It was Diane Mathieson I spoke to and she said to stop Costello, I really had to make it official, so yes in the end I did report her for harassment.'

Anderson nodded, imagining how that conversation would have gone down. He was about to ask if Costello had left him alone after that but Haggerty returned to talking about Mary Jane. Anderson had thought he had caught a moment's hesitation, when Haggerty had considered lying, lying as an afterthought. Haggerty was here to talk his own conversation; the mention of Costello had made him a little uneasy, scared even.

Had she been onto something?

He sipped his coffee, watching as George Haggerty rubbed Moses' head and for the first time Colin Anderson felt a little fearful of what might have become of his sidekick.

He dragged away the chair, pulling Moses' cot with it.

The Casualty officer had taken one quick look, checked the chart where the patient's vital signs were being recorded and then taken a closer look at the occipital wound. While noticing it was remarkably clean, he saw it was also very deep. Any pressure with his fingers caused the patient to pull away but not before he had felt a degree of cushioning under his fingertips. He needed an X-ray to confirm what he already knew:

there was a fracture in there. The woman was sitting on an examination couch. Hannah had patted the pillow, and gestured in every way that she could think of, but the woman remained sitting.

'She might not want to lie down with a head wound like that, and I don't blame her. Can you get an X-ray organized? It takes a hard blow to fracture an occiput, but I don't like the feel of it. If we see a fracture, we will MRI. Or if her neurologicals start to decline. They are fine at the moment but her comprehension's slow and she's not verbalizing. Not in any language. Weird. Keep her under close observation. Stay with her, go with her to Radiology. Let me know if anything changes.' The woman was co-operative but he noticed she had latched onto Hannah, her eyes flicking back and forth. When he asked a question, the woman would look to Hannah for an indication as to whether the answer was yes or no. And then let Hannah answer for both of them.

The doctor left, Hannah heard him talking to the cops, then heard them ask where the nearest vending machine was.

Hannah talked constantly, explaining to the patient that she needed to undress in case they needed a scan later and offered her a gown so she could examine her for other injuries, old scars, stitch marks that might show the site of a metal implant. The woman was co-operative, not really following instructions but not resisting as Hannah opened the zip of the anorak and slipped the woman's arms out. It was soaking wet and stank of alcohol. She held it under her nose, the smell was overwhelming, leaving Hannah to wonder if somebody had smashed a bottle of plonk over the back of her head. She'd seen that before.

Hannah leant over the patient to slip her arms out the wet jumper; had she got wet through the anorak? Had she been somewhere without her jacket? Hannah breathed in over the patient's hair. It smelled of shampoo, coconut shampoo. She sniffed at the patient's breath as she looked into her eyes. No alcohol.

Hannah leaned forward again as she undid the top buttons of the black jumper, checking. Definitely no smell of drink on her breath. She stood back and looked at her, something

here wasn't right. Then she put her head out the cubicle and
requested a plastic bag for the woman's belongings. The
woman watched as her arms were revealed from the sleeves
of the jumper, cold, pink skin with lacerations, cuts on the
lower forearms, defensive wounds. The arms had been held
up to ward off an attack to the head. Yet the clothes were
intact? No tears in the fabric of the T-shirt, jumper or anorak.

'Good God,' said Hannah, now thinking about sexual assault
and that the victim had been undressed then redressed. 'What
the hell has happened to you?' She looked into the grey eyes.
They stared back at her, something was rumbling around in
there at the back of the patient's head. 'Can I take your T-shirt
off?' There was no obedience, but no resistance. Hannah rolled
up the T-shirt, starting at the waist. The patient winced,
flinching a little so Hannah apologized and leaned forward to
look over the patient's shoulder to her back.

'Shit!' She let the T-shirt fall back down and hurriedly stuck
her head out the curtain to get hold of the two cops. Their
seats were empty.

Anderson eventually guided George Haggerty on to the terrace,
the elegant façade lit up in bright amber, two windows already
showing the sprinkling lights of early Christmas trees. Anderson
breathed in the cold night air, the rain had stopped.

'How long does it take you to drive up there? Up to Port
MacDuff.' He looked at his watch.

'Five and a half hours? Thereabouts. The A9 is forty miles
longer but six minutes quicker, if I don't get stopped for
speeding. I thought the average speed cameras had put an end
to that. Bastards.' Then George remembered who he was
talking to. 'Sorry.'

'They are bastards. Even we can't stand them.'

'Well, look on the bright side, if I hadn't got nicked for
speeding you would still think that I was involved in my wife's
death, my son's death.'

'Every cloud.'

They had reached the back of the Volvo, but George
Haggerty made no attempt to unlock the car. 'Have you not
heard from Costello?'

'Nope, not at all.' Anderson shook his head, hands in his pockets.

'I saw her on the 8th. She called me on the 11th . . .' Haggerty rubbed his chin. 'Friday? Saturday? Definitely Saturday. Didn't say much, just told me that I wouldn't get away with it. Must have been Saturday. I was talking to the estate agent when she phoned.'

Anderson couldn't hide his curiosity. 'Did she say anything else?'

'Just the usual abuse,' Haggerty said, good-naturedly.

'Estate agent? Are you selling the house?' Anderson's shiver was nothing to do with the chill of the night air.

'Oh, there's no way I can go back and live there, not after that. I've said to Valerie to go out and see if she wants anything, but me? No.' He shook his head. He got his keys out his pocket and beeped the boot open. 'Do you think it got to your colleague in the end, the way she found the bodies? The scene was brutal.'

It was on the tip of his tongue to say, well she has seen worse. But he didn't know if that was true, but Costello felt guilty, and had ranted about the way Malcolm, according to her, had been so desperate to get away from his father he had tried to climb out the window. Anderson could see both sides. Children can cultivate anybody who will listen. Malcolm had lost his elder sister, he must have known about the attack on Valerie. His life was already unsettled and then . . . well. Then what?

Haggerty nodded. 'Well, if you see her . . .' he laughed. 'Tell her I'm innocent, OK?' The smile switched off as fast as it had switched on. 'I know she's your colleague, ex-colleague.'

'I know you have complained, but she hasn't been sacked.' Anderson nodded; the chill of the night was starting to gnaw at his bones now. 'You got your picture?' he asked, pointing to the package under Haggerty's arm.

'Yes. My dad will be thrilled. He can't believe it. A great-grandson.'

Except he isn't, thought Anderson, nodding. Good manners made him provide the expected response. 'Well, if he is ever down this way then give me a call, and we can get them together and he can see Moses for himself.'

Haggerty opened the boot of his car, the light came on and he swung his bag and the picture into the boot. The back of the car was illuminated to show it crammed full of bags and boxes, piled on top of an offcut of orange carpet, a tarp covering the back of the boot so it was kept very clean. Of course, he was clearing out his house. He reached for something packed safely at the back.

'I hope you don't mind but I came across this and I thought you might like it. Just one of those things.' He handed over a flat package wrapped in bubble wrap. Anderson unpeeled the padding and as he did, his fingers felt the regular squares, the widened border. It was a photo frame and as he unwound the wrapping, the photograph came into view. He didn't need to ask who it was. The girl in the picture looked very like Claire, lighter colouring, but the same smile, and though Anderson knew Mary Jane had been seven years older than Claire, in this picture, she looked so much younger.

Fresh faced, hair uncoloured and falling naturally round her face. The rain spotted the glass as he held it there, she became more interesting behind the pinpoints of rain water, they added an ethereal quality to her smile.

'Mary Jane, about sixteen or seventeen then.'

'Yeah, a good kid before she lost her dad,' said Haggerty. 'My good friend Oscar. And that was horrible. He sailed off, he drowned. All the coastguard found were bits of burning wreckage. The dinghy was still tied to the *Jennifer Rhu*. And if the wee boat was still tied to the yacht, he didn't get off the burning boat. You can understand the effect that had on Abby and Mary Jane, seven years of wrangling to get him declared dead, as there was no body. It was a horrible time, absolutely bloody awful. Mary Jane grew up through all that.'

It was the most animated Anderson had ever seen him.

Haggerty said, opening the door and climbing into the car, 'She didn't have a father, you know. She had three and none of us were there when it mattered.'

And with that he indicated and pulled out into the terrace.

She didn't have a father, you know.

What did Haggerty actually mean by that?

Oscar Duguid had died years before Anderson had any idea